CHINESE FOLK STORY

The Banana Child

Collected by Xiao Ganniu
Adapted by Bao Guangman
Illustrated by Long Niannan

DOLPHIN BOOKS   BEIJING

First Edition   1987

Hard Cover: ISBN 0-8351-1891-6
Paperback: ISBN 0-8351-1892-4

Copyright 1987 by Dolphin Books

Published by Dolphin Books
24 Baiwanzhuang Road, Beijing, China
Distributed by China International Book Trading Corporation
(Guoji Shudian), P.O. Box 399, Beijing, China

Printed in the People's Republic of China

A long, long time ago there lived an old hunchbacked man who had no children. He lived alone and longed for a child.

He grew banana plants on the hill. They grew luxuriantly and yielded lots of bananas.

When the bananas were ripe, he would pick them and take them to
market to sell them.

With the money he earned, he bought rice, salt, oil, and other things he needed, and then he came home.

One year an unexpected snow and a fierce north wind damaged all his banana plants.

The old man shed sad tears at the sight of the damaged plants.

The next spring only one banana plant had sprouted.

He watered and fertilized the single plant diligently, and it grew fast.
Very soon it bore a banana — only one, but a very big one.

The banana grew bigger and bigger until it was as thick as a water barrel.

One day the skin of banana broke, and in the centre sat a plump child!

The hunchbacked man was delighted and called him his Banana Child. On hearing this, the child replied sweetly: "Papa."

When the child grew big and strong enough, he helped his papa do some housework.

As time went on, the old man's back bent over more and more, until it looked just like a bow.

The Banana Child could not endure seeing his father's poor health. One day he said to his father, "Papa, I want to go out to look for a medicine to cure your back."

The Banana Child wandered everywhere and asked many people where the medicine was, but nobody could tell him about it.

Though he wore out the soles of his shoes and then the uppers, he did not give up but went on looking for it.

One day he met a maiden who was combing her long hair by a stream.

"Sister," he said to her, "I have come a long way and experienced many hardships to look for the medicine to cure my father's back, but I cannot find it. Would you be kind enough to tell me where it is?"

The maiden believed that he was a good child, for he was not afraid of hardships to help his father.

So the maiden told him that in the cave of the East Mountain there was a pearl which could cure any illness.

The Banana Child went to the East Mountain, climbed into the cave, and found the pearl.

On his way home he saw a child cowherd crying.

It happened that one of his bulls had broken the child's arm when he tried to stop it from fighting with another bull.

On hearing this, the Banana Child put the pearl into the cowherd's mouth. Very soon a strange thing happened — his broken arm got well again.

Afterwards the Banana Child went to look for the long-haired maiden again. This time she told him that there was a white mushroom on the top of the West Mountain and that it could also cure any kind of illness.

The Banana Child climbed up the West Mountain and picked the white mushroom that was growing there.

On his way home he saw an old man lying on the ground with his leg broken by a fallen tree.

The Banana Child pushed the tree away and put the mushroom into the old man's mouth. His leg was cured right away.

The Banana Child went to look for the maiden again, and she told him that in the pond at the foot of the South Mountain there was a golden stone which could also cure any illness.

The Banana Child was about to leave when the maiden stopped him, saying, "Little boy, don't come again. Those three treasures are the only ones I know."

The child nodded and left. At the foot of the South Mountain he jumped into the water and got the golden stone.

On his way home he heard the sound of crying from under a bridge. It was a woman who had fallen off the bridge and hurt herself.

The Banana Child put the golden stone into her mouth. As soon as he did so, she jumped up and was well again.

Now the Banana Child got home bare-handed. He told his father the whole story. "That's all right," said his father, praising him. "You did exactly what I expect you to do."

While they were talking, a little peacock flew overhead.

The peacock shook its head, wagged its tail, and turned into a maiden.

The Banana Child looked at her carefully and saw that she was the fairy maiden with the long hair who had helped him. The maiden fetched a bowl of magic water and gave it to the old man to drink.

The hunchbacked old man drank it up, and soon he stood up straight and tall. From then on the maiden lived happily with the old man and his son.

中国民间故事

香 蕉 娃 娃

肖甘牛　整理

鲍光满　改编

龙念南　绘画

*

海豚出版社出版

（中国北京百万庄路24号）

人教印刷厂印刷

中国国际图书贸易总公司

（中国国际书店）发行

北京399信箱

1987年（20开）第一版

编号：（英）8482—160

00500（精）

00290（平）

88—E—357